PAUL KROPP

AMY'S WISH

EMC Publishing, St. Paul, Minnesota

Encounters Series Titles

Burn Out	Dead On	Gang War	Micro Man
Dope Deal	Dirt Bike	Wild One	The Beast
Runaway	No Way	Snow Ghost	Spin Out
Hot Cars	Fair Play	Baby Baby	Amy's Wish

Encounters Series Teacher's Guides are also available.

Library of Congress Cataloging in·Publication Data

Kropp, Paul.
　Amy's wish.

　(Encounters series)
　Summary: A depressed girl is brought to an appreciation
of the value of life by a friend suffering from leukemia.
　[1. Leukemia—Fiction. 2. Friendship—Fiction.
3. Life—Fiction] I. Title. II.
Series: Kropp, Paul. Encounters series.

PZ7.K93Am　1986　[Fic]　　　　　　　85-6951
ISBN 0-8219-0168-0

Published by EMC Publishing
300 York Avenue
St. Paul, Minnesota 55101

0　9　8　7　6　5　4

CONTENTS

CHAPTER

I sat all alone at the Halloween party, curled up by myself in a corner. Everybody else was having a great time. A bunch of kids danced to music that came pounding out of the stereo. Some guy with a gross mask was telling a joke to Amy. Bennie and the stoners had their own group in the other room while the brainers were all playing mind games on the porch. Most of the kids had funny costumes on. I was dressed up like a witch.

I had a drink in one hand and a cigarette in the other. The drink was awful, even worse than our Chicago water, and the cigarette was worse. I kept hoping that the booze would make me feel better, but it didn't.

It had been an awful week—at home, at school, everywhere. My father had been slugging back the beer worse than ever. My older brother kept treating me like some kind of moron. And Paul, well, that was all over.

So I sat alone in the corner, feeling sad and lonely and sick. I felt as if there were a wall between me and the rest of the world. I was on my side of the wall, all alone. The world was on the other side of it, dancing and having a good time.

Then it got even worse. I saw Paul come in the front door—with *her*. He had his arm around her waist and they were smiling and laughing just like everybody else.

Paul was dressed in the same prince costume that he had worn with me to last year's party, but now he had a new princess.

And me? I was nothing but a lousy old witch, curled up in the corner.

Watching Paul and his new girlfriend really made me feel down. I hated him and I hated myself—all at once.

But I didn't get angry. That's the strange part, when I look back on it. I've always been a fighter, a girl who'd rather get into trouble than chicken out of it. Some people even say that I'm tough, but that only shows how much they know. Inside I hurt just like other people, maybe even more than they do. Inside I'm a mess.

"What's the matter, Karen?"

I looked up and saw my friend Amy looking down at me. She smiled and that helped a little. There was at least one other person on my side of the wall.

"I'm fine," I lied.

"You don't look it," Amy said, even before she saw Paul over by the door. "Oh, I think I'm getting the reason. It's Prince Charming over there, isn't it?"

"He's only part of it," I said, and that was the truth. "Nobody wants a stupid old witch, anyhow."

"Karen, you've got to stop being so down on yourself. There are a lot of guys in school who are interested in you. Why,

some guy in the other room was asking about you just now."

"Yeah, Bennie—maybe he wants to sell me some dope."

"Not like that," Amy shook her head. "Look, even if you're not interested in him, there's a bunch of guys on the porch...."

"I don't want to play any games with the brainers. I want to ... get drunk," I told her. That wasn't really the truth, but it's what I said. The truth was that I didn't know exactly what I wanted.

"Karen, don't be like that," Amy said,

sitting down beside me.

"You go find Eric and have some fun," I said. "I'll stay here and make some magic spells and be just fine."

"You should dance," Amy said.

"I don't want to. I'm going to turn Paul into a toad and his new princess into a worm and my father into a mushroom. You go ahead and enjoy yourself, all right?"

"Well, O.K., but I'll be back later," she said, getting to her feet. A second later and she was swallowed up in the party.

Then I was sorry I had sent her away. I had felt better talking to someone, but sitting by myself I started thinking about my problems again. They all seemed so awful and there was just no escape for me. I needed some way out from everything that was messing up my life, but there was no way out that I could see. There was only more of the same—pain, hurt, sadness.

I felt like I was going to be sick. I could see Amy and Eric dancing, looking only at each other. Paul and I had been like that, once, and remembering those nights made me feel sad.

I got slowly to my feet and stumbled
up to the second floor bathroom. When I
closed the bathroom door behind me, I
only felt worse. I was sick, but I couldn't
throw up. I felt trapped in my life, but I
couldn't escape. I held my head in my
hands and tried to snap out of it, but I
couldn't.

And then it came to me. There was a
razor sitting on the ledge over the
bathtub. I looked at the razor and I knew
that I could use it as a way out of my
whole rotten life. A few deep cuts and I
could escape.

12

Then they'd see. Then everyone would have to understand.

It was a scary idea, of course. Maybe that was one of the reasons I liked it so much. Someone would find me before I died and get me fixed up. And even if nobody found me in time, would that be so bad?

I started to think about what it would be like. In my dream I was at my own funeral, watching all the people who would come to say good-bye. I could see myself lying there, dead, in the coffin. All my friends would be there. Paul would be there, too, and he'd feel awful. He'd remember the fun times we used to have before it all went rotten—and he'd feel guilty. That was the part I really liked.

My father would be standing beside the coffin. He'd finally see that he demanded too much of me. Of course he'd be crying. Maybe he'd even be sober for a change. My brother would be standing next to my father, having to do all the work now that I was gone. My brother would feel bad about the way he had treated me, but it would be too late for him to say that he was sorry. It

would be too late for all of them.

I got the razor blade out and held it in my fingers. The steel was cold and the idea of using it suddenly scared me. It would hurt. I might really die. They might not find me in time. All these crazy thoughts kept running through my mind as I held the blade tightly in my fingers.

Then somebody rattled the bathroom door. I froze. A voice called out, "Hurry up in there."

It was Paul! He'd be the one to find me—he'd be the one to break down the bathroom door and see me lying on the floor. Then he'd rush in and hold me, for the very last time. And he'd never, ever forget.

That made up my mind. I put my right arm over the sink and got ready. This was the time to do it—now, right now.

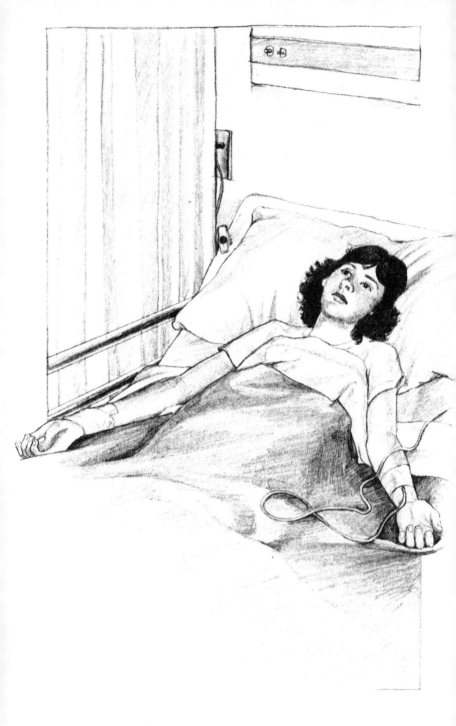

CHAPTER

2

When I first opened my eyes, I couldn't remember what had happened. I was lying in a hospital bed and the bright lights overhead hurt my eyes. There were curtains around my bed, so I couldn't see the people moving around outside. Somewhere there were machines that made a humming noise.

I thought for a second that I was still asleep and in the middle of a dream. Then it all came rushing back into my mind—the party, the razor blade, all that blood. I tried to sit up, but I felt too weak to move. Then, turning my head to one side, I saw Amy sitting on a chair beside the bed.

"Karen?" she asked, maybe wondering if I was really awake.

"How did I get here?" I asked her. My mouth felt dry as sandpaper.

"Eric's dad drove you here to the hospital after they took the bathroom door off. When they carried you out, you looked so white... and I was so scared," Amy said, breaking into tears.

I didn't know what to tell her. I felt so ashamed. Here was Amy, sitting beside me, with tears rolling down her

cheeks and blood stains on her new sweater. I wanted to say something to make her feel better. I wanted to say that I was sorry, that it was all a mistake. But I couldn't. Instead I rolled over in bed and curled up into a ball. I listened to the sound of the hospital. It seemed to breathe like a giant animal. I could hear the crying and coughing from other beds beyond the curtain, from people hurt in other ways.

I thought back to what had happened at the party. It all came back to me with feelings of pain and guilt and shame.

How stupid I was! Imagine thinking that suicide was a way out, that it would somehow make Paul care about me or help me get back at my father. And how could I do something like that to Amy, to the one person who really did care about me?

"Karen Fowler," a voice said. I turned in the bed and saw a woman standing in the doorway. She was a small, grey-haired woman who looked very tired. "I'm Dr. Vitucci, part of the psychology team here."

"I don't need a shrink," I told her,

pulling the blankets up over my head.

Everything was so awful. I wanted to forget the party and the blood—I wanted to act as if nothing had happened. I just felt so stupid and embarrassed, but I couldn't tell that to a stranger. I couldn't even say it all to Amy.

"I think she's still upset," Amy told the shrink.

Upset! I was a lot more than upset. I was sick and ashamed and I felt like a total fool.

I had wanted to get back at all the rotten people in my life. I had wanted to show my father that I couldn't stand him any more. I had wanted to show Paul how much he had hurt me. I had wanted out—out of everything—and now I was lying in a scratchy hospital bed, feeling even worse than before.

"Karen, I need to get a few facts for the hospital report," the doctor said.

"I just want to be left alone," I told her.

"And you must be her friend . . . ?" she asked.

"Yes, my name is Amy Daler and I've known Karen since we were in fifth grade. Karen and I play softball . . . well, I guess you don't really need to know all that," Amy told her.

I didn't say a word. I wanted the shrink to go stuff her papers someplace and leave me alone.

"I was wondering if there has been any attempt at suicide before this," Dr. Vitucci said.

"None of your business," I told her.

Amy shook her head. "No, Karen's never done anything to . . . hurt herself."

"Is that true, Karen?" the doctor asked me.

"I don't have to answer that," I shot back at her.

"That's right, Karen, you don't *have* to answer anything," the shrink began. "You can just keep all your problems hidden deep, down inside you. You can just walk out of the hospital and tell yourself that all this was a little mistake and it won't happen again. But it's not as simple as that, Karen, and you're smart enough to know that. I want to help you, so something like this won't happen again— but I can't do anything if you won't even talk to me."

I pulled the blanket down so that I could see her. Dr. Vitucci and Amy were both looking at me, worried about me. I felt like a little kid who's been caught doing something stupid and rotten. I was embarrassed and upset—and I was taking it all out on them.

"She's just trying to help," Amy said.

"I'm sorry," I whispered, suddenly having to fight back tears. "I'll tell you what you need to know."

"Thank you, Karen," the doctor said. "Now, I have a feeling that something happened at the party that got you very upset. Am I right?"

"It was everything," I told her, "not just the party."

Amy broke in, "There was one thing, though. Karen and her boyfriend split up a week ago and he showed up at the party with another girl."

"I didn't do it just because of him," I said, too ashamed to admit even part of the truth.

"Do you think it might be one reason?" the doctor asked.

"Well, maybe," I admitted.

"Karen, you said before that everything was getting you down," Dr. Vitucci said. "What else would be part of that 'everything'?"

"School . . . my father . . . I don't even know where to start," I told her. "Do we really have to talk about it right now?"

"That's fine—let me set up a time to see you and your father next week," Dr. Vitucci said.

"You won't tell him what I did, will you?" I asked.

"He already knows, Karen. The man who drove you in already called your house. Your brother said that your dad

would be here soon to take you home."

I tried to keep in control of myself, to pretend I didn't care. But then I fell apart and started crying.

"I don't want to see him," I cried. "Can't you keep me in here for a day... or something, anything?"

"Karen, you have to face your father sooner or later," the doctor said. "Do it now, with the two of us here to support you, and you'll find it a lot easier."

I knew that she was right. There was nothing I could do to avoid him or the awful thing I had done.

A short time later, a nurse told me my father was in the waiting room, ready to take me home. Amy helped me to get my stuff together. Then she and the shrink walked with me to where my father was standing. For a second, no one said a word. Then my father opened his mouth.

"Karen, how could you do something like this?"

I looked up and saw all the anger in his eyes, as if I had hurt him even more than I had hurt myself. And then I broke down, crying on Amy's shoulder.

CHAPTER

It was awful at home. Somehow I had to put up with two of my biggest problems—my father and my brother.

My brother Kevin has always acted like he's Mr. Wonderful, while I'm some reject who couldn't really be his sister. When I saw him the next day, he had a sick smile on his face. His smile said what he wouldn't dare say in words—*you can't get anything right, can you?*

But he wouldn't give me any excuse to blow up at him or to punch him in his stupid buck teeth. Instead, he pretended to care. He said that he was concerned

about me. It was enough to make me
sick.

My father, on the other hand, didn't
even pretend. He tried to ignore what I
had done just like he ignored everything
else I did. He didn't want to talk about it,
or accept the fact that it had happened.

Instead, he drank. The beer was gone
so he started hitting the whisky. And
when the whisky was gone . . . well,
anything from mouthwash on up would
do.

After a weekend of my father's
bloodshot eyes and my brother's sick

smile, I was looking forward to school on Monday. But school turned out to be a horror story all by itself. I could tell it would be an awful day as soon as I walked up the school steps. Kids who knew me looked away—and the jerks who didn't know me just stared.

Everybody knew!

I don't know why I was surprised, since the fifty people at the party must each have told the story to fifty more. But now I really was a freak. Some people might pretend not to look, but I knew that they wanted to stare like everybody else. *There's the girl who tried to kill herself at Eric's party! Oh, how gross!*

I looked around for Amy, but she wasn't by the doors where she usually met me. I waited a little while for her, but that meant letting the whole school stare at me as they went inside. At last I couldn't take the stares and went by myself. I was ashamed enough. I didn't need every dumb kid in the school to make it worse for me.

At my locker, I talked with a girl from my homeroom class. She was the

first person to ask how I was, and her concern made me feel better. But by third class, I was so sick of "How are you?" that I was ready to throw up.

Even the teachers knew. Old Mrs. Winters had called me Carol all term because her brain had dried up thirty years ago—but that day she got my name right. During her math class, she kept looking at me like I was some poor, sick child.

I hated it. People were talking all around me, but I felt singled out and very alone. I felt that the wall between me and the world was building up again, one block at a time. But I couldn't tell anyone how I really felt until I saw Amy at lunch.

"Where were you?" I asked when I saw her. I was angry about being left on my own that morning.

"At the hospital," she said in a tired voice.

"Talking to Dr. Vitucci about me?" I asked, just teasing, really.

"No, Karen. Maybe you're not the only person around here who's got a problem."

I was surprised by the serious way she spoke. "What's the matter, then?" I asked her.

"Oh, something's wrong with my blood, so the doctors are doing some tests."

"I told you not to make out with Herb Kline. That guy is a walking disease," I said, still teasing her. Amy had never really made out with anybody, at least not until Eric came along.

"Cut the jokes, Karen," she said, not even smiling. "The real question is how are *you* doing today?"

"I'm going to scream," I told her.

"Not here in the cafeteria," Amy said, maybe because I had pulled that stunt before.

"No, I'm going to scream if one more person asks me how I am. I'll tell you how I am—I want to crawl in some hole and hide. You'd think I was the only kid in Chicago who ever . . . you know."

"Well, people care about you."

"People think I'm a freak," I told her.

"You shouldn't talk like that . . . oh, oh—here comes Paul," Amy said, her voice dropping to a whisper.

I wished I could hide so he couldn't see me. I just didn't want to face him, not now, not on my first day back.

Paul walked past our table, his eyes looking way off toward the corner. He was trying so hard not to see me that I knew he had taken a good long look.

"He's gone over to sit with Greg Norton and those other rejects," Amy said after he had passed by. "I'll never know why you fell for a jerk like that."

"Maybe a jerk like that is all I deserve," I told her.

"Would you stop talking like that?"

Amy snapped at me. "That's what got you so upset at the party. You start looking down on yourself and you forget what life is all about. I still can't believe what you did just to get back at Paul."

"I know, but...."

I couldn't finish what I started to say. After the awful morning at school, and Paul, and now Amy lecturing me, I was ready to cry my head off.

"I'm sorry," Amy said, reading all that in my face. "I didn't mean to make things worse than they already are. Isn't it better being here at school than home with your father?"

"A toss-up, I think."

"Well, maybe things will get better after you two go to the shrink on Wednesday."

"It'll be good for him," I said.

"Maybe it'll be good for you, too," Amy answered.

I started to eat my sandwich and Amy didn't say anything more. The silence between us seemed strange, since there was so much that we had to talk about. I had the feeling that Amy was trying to say something important, but having trouble finding the right words. At last she went ahead—

"Karen, I know you're having a pretty tough time right now, so maybe I shouldn't ask you about this today. But I was hoping you'd do me one favor."

"What do you want?"

"Make me a promise," Amy said, "a promise that you won't try it again."

Amy stared right at me, her blue eyes begging me to say yes, but I couldn't. Any promise that I gave her would have been a lie. Nothing important in my life had changed and a lot of things were

getting worse.

"Promise you won't?" Amy asked again.

"I can't promise that, Amy... I just can't."

CHAPTER

My father and I went back to the hospital on Wednesday to see the shrink. I don't think either of us really wanted to go. There was something embarrassing about going to a shrink. It's like hanging your problems on a clothesline where the whole world can see them. Yet I had told Amy that I'd go and my father was ready to go through the motions. Deep down, I think he was scared that I would try it again. Deep down, so was I.

The shrink was in an office marked Staff Psychologist. I thought that meant the walls would be padded. But I was wrong, of course—no padded walls, no shock stuff, nothing like that. The office was as boring as the waiting room at a dentist's.

Dr. Vitucci came in wearing one of those white lab coats and a tag with her name on it. She gave us your standard doctor's smile—sort of, *You're sick and I'm well.* My father smiled back and showed off his rotten teeth. I was just afraid that somebody had seen me come into the office. The kids at school already thought I was a freak. I didn't want to be a nut-case as well.

"I'm glad to see the two of you here," Dr. Vitucci began.

I'm not glad to be here, I thought, but I didn't say it. Instead I stared out the window at Taylor Field.

"I'm just hoping that you can help Karen," my father said. "I've done the best that I can trying to raise her, but I guess that wasn't enough."

I had heard that kind of line from him before—my father, the man who tries so hard. I felt my stomach turning over. Why didn't my father tell her who did all the cooking, who did the laundry,

who paid the taxi drivers when they brought him home from bars, drunk out of his mind. It sure wasn't my brother. Of course, my father would never give *me* any credit.

"Karen," Dr. Vitucci said, "what problems do you think led up to last Friday?"

"I don't know," I said, thinking that *she* ought to be telling *me*.

"It was that kid Paul, if you ask me," my father said, jumping in. "I should have stopped the two of them a year ago when it all began."

"Mr. Fowler," the doctor said, "I'd like to get Karen's feelings."

That shut my father up—but good.

"There were a lot of things," I admitted, "but Paul was only one of them. I guess I should have known all along that he was going to dump me, but I didn't know how much it would hurt."

"If her mother were still alive," my father said, "she could have talked to Karen about these things. How could I know how upset she was?"

"What else was there, Karen? You said

there were lots of things," Dr. Vitucci asked me.

"The same as everybody else, I guess. In school the kids think I'm sort of weird and that gets me down. And I don't see my best friend Amy that much now that she's got a boyfriend, so I guess I've felt kind of lonely."

"Anything at home, Karen?"

"Well...." I felt funny talking about that in front of my father. I'd hardly know where to start, anyway.

"Karen used to be easy to get along with before her mother died," my father said, breaking in again. "Since then, there have been problems between us. She was twelve and going through all those changes...and then the loss of her mother. Well, we've all had to work harder since then, but I don't think Karen is too happy about her jobs around the house now."

"But I do them, don't I? That's more than you can say about Kevin."

"You see what I mean, doctor?" he said, shooting a look at Dr. Vitucci. He was trying to blame everything on me again.

"Why don't you tell her who does all the cooking and cleaning up?" I asked, raising my voice. "You think I'm some sort of slave who ought to spend all my time looking after you. Well, I spend a lot of time doing that, and you're still not happy. All I ever hear around the house is 'Karen, do this, Karen, do that.' It's enough to make me sick," I told him.

Oh, there was more, much more that I could have said, but I stopped short. I was ashamed to be talking like this in front of a stranger.

"It's been like this between us ever

since her mother died," my father said, staring angrily at me. "I still think the shock of that has a lot to do with Karen's problem."

"I'm not sure it's fair to call it just Karen's problem, Mr. Fowler," the doctor said.

"But you don't understand—Karen's mother killed herself," he said.

"That's a lie," I shot back. It was a lie—it had to be a lie.

"But it's the truth, Karen," my father went on. "Nobody would mix pills like that unless... well, you know what it means."

"What does it mean to you?" Dr. Vitucci asked him.

"It means that she couldn't handle her problems and took the quick way out. Now I see the same thing happening in Karen," he said.

"You're making everything up," I told him. "Mom wouldn't have done that—she loved us too much to do that. Her death ... it was an accident."

"It was suicide, Karen. You can't keep on hiding from the truth."

"It's not the truth—it's a lie you made

up as an excuse for your drinking."

"There—you see what I've had to put up with," my father said.

I'd had all I could take from him.

"Don't you listen to him," I shouted to the doctor. "He twists everything his own way. He's the one who needs help—not me."

I was crying now, tears falling down my face while I stood up and tried to think of what to do.

I felt trapped by my father's lies, by everything. Nobody could understand what it was like to live with him. Nobody would ever know what I had to put up with.

"Karen, please sit down," Dr. Vitucci said, trying to calm me.

"No, I don't want to listen to his lies and how tough it's been for him and all that...I can't take it any more."

I ran from the office, slamming the door behind me. All I knew then was that I had to escape—and that I'd never go back. Never.

CHAPTER

After a week, the bandage came off my wrist. The scar from the cut wasn't that bad. If you really looked at my wrist— well, you might guess what had happened. But who looks at wrists?

At school, I finally got over the feeling that I was a freak. The kids stopped whispering about me and went back to talking about concerts, the Black Hawks, and just how stoned so-and-so got at a party.

At home, it was a different story. I didn't talk to my father after our fight at the shrink's. This didn't stop him from getting drunk and ordering me around. Nor did it stop my brother from telling me I had acted like a child.

I tried to tough all this out, but inside I was hurting. I knew that the problems that had messed me up before were still there—and about to become worse.

I was putting lights on the Christmas tree when the telephone rang. It was Amy, saying that she needed to talk to me. Something about the shaky tone in her voice told me that she was in trouble. But I didn't know then how bad the trouble was.

When Amy met me at the door to her house, I could see right away that she was upset. She looked awful—her face was pale and her eyes were red from crying.

"You look pretty ragged," I said. "Did you have a fight with Eric?"

"No, worse," she told me.

"Sounds like *really* bad news," I said before taking out a cigarette.

"Yeah...," Amy began, almost as if she wanted to tell me something, but couldn't find the words.

I could hardly believe this was the same person who'd been joking and laughing with me the week before.

"Amy, what is it?" I asked. "You haven't acted like this since we lost that big softball game last summer."

"Well, at least you won't lose any games next season because of me," she said, trying to smile.

"What do you mean? You can't quit the team."

"It's not up to me, Karen. You see, I went to the doctor today—" she began. There were tears in her voice, so she stopped to get control back.

I was scared. I began putting two-and-two together—her tired feeling, the way she looked, the hospital tests. I was afraid of what it might add up to.

"Tell me it's mono, will you?" I said, not wanting to hear what was coming.

"It's not, Karen—it's cancer," she whispered.

I went to her and held her, held her close. I didn't know what to say. *Cancer.* Cancer was such a frightening word that it just couldn't be real. Cancer happened to old people, to people that you heard about, not to kids like us.

But that's what Amy had said. And now everything was spinning in my mind—all these awful pictures of pain and slow death.

"When did the doctor tell you?" I asked. I was wondering how long she had known and tried to face it all by herself.

"Just this morning, but I think he had an idea that it was cancer last week, and so did I. The doctor didn't want to say anything until all the tests were done."

"So he's sure?" I asked, hoping that the answer would be no.

"He wouldn't have told me unless it was certain. I've been worrying about it all this time, but I didn't want to tell you—because of all your problems at home."

"That's no reason not to tell me when something is bothering you," I said to her.

"Well, I didn't want to tell you what I was most afraid of—and that turned out to be what I've got."

"So are they going to do an operation?" I asked.

"They can't, Karen. It's leukemia...
the cancer is in my blood."

"Oh, no," I whispered. I had read
about leukemia and I knew that all the
odds were against her.

"I start chemotherapy on Friday and
the doctor says it's going to be really
tough. I was thinking about it all day,
wondering if it was going to be worth it.
Sometimes they can catch it and keep the
cancer under control, but most of the
time...."

"You can't just give up, Amy," I told
her.

I wasn't thinking then how strange
those words must sound, coming from
me.

"I know," she said, shaking her head.
"But I don't feel good and all the worry
has made me tired. I'll be O.K. in the
morning, I guess, but right now I just
feel so down."

I tried to find some words to make
her feel better, but everything I thought
of seemed to sound stupid.

"You know the worst part?" Amy
went on. "I'm going to lose my hair. It's
funny because I never much liked my

hair. It gets all greasy in the summer and always looks stupid under a baseball cap. And now, well, I think I'm going to miss it."

Amy looked at me and smiled sadly for a second.

"Oh, Karen, I'm so afraid I'm going to look like a freak," she said, breaking into tears.

"It'll be O.K.," I told her, hugging her as she cried.

I was trying very hard to keep my own tears back.

"You can get a wig until it starts

growing back. Why, you can have red hair or purple or even green hair if you want."

"Sure," she said, smiling a little.

"And whenever you feel bad, all you have to do is call me and I'll—"

"Call me baldie," she finished for me.

"Yeah, and I'll remind you of the time your bathing suit came off while you were water-skiing."

"That's going to cheer me up?" Amy asked.

"Sure it will," I told her, trying to show a lot more hope than I really felt. "How does this chemotherapy work? I mean, do you have to go in the hospital?"

"Well, I won't be in all the time, maybe a couple days a week. The chemo is really a poison that they put in your blood to kill the cancer. The trouble is that the poison will get to the rest of me too and make me moody and really sick."

"How long does the chemo last?" I asked her.

"A few months right now, then maybe a few months more if they don't catch it the first time."

Amy told me the facts about her cancer and what was going to happen, and all the talking seemed to help. Maybe that's how it is—maybe that's what facts are for.

By the time I left, it was after midnight. Amy was very, very tired, but I think she felt better after talking to me. She stopped looking at the odds against her and started looking at what she had to do to stay alive. That was the important thing.

Amy's dad offered to drive me home, but I said I wanted to walk by myself. I had so much to think about.

All night I had tried to be cheerful to give Amy strength when she was down, but the talk had taken a toll on me. I was sad and angry at the same time. I wasn't angry at anybody or anything— just at the way life was.

One week before Christmas and my best friend learns she has cancer. The more I thought about that, the more I gritted my teeth in anger.

"It's not fair," I cried out into the night. "It's not fair!"

CHAPTER

All through the winter, I tried to see
Amy every day. When she was feeling
well enough to come to school, I laughed
and joked with her just like always.
When she had to stay at home, I brought
work from school to her house.

Amy suffered through it all—the
sickness, the mood changes, even the loss
of her hair. But the cancer was still
inside her, like an enemy army that had
taken over her blood. I watched as Amy
became weaker and weaker, until her
parents couldn't take care of her at home
any more. When Amy went into the

hospital, it was a shock to us all.

On the days when she was really sick, I'd talk to her about the summer and how we'd start playing baseball again. I tried hard to be cheerful, to give her hope when she felt down.

But, to tell the truth, I didn't have much hope. Of course, I kept my fear hidden, since Amy's battle against cancer was hard enough already. But in my own mind, the future looked awful.

I guess it was this lack of hope deep down inside me that set me up for Bennie. That was the really stupid thing. When you give up on life, then you're almost certain to get hurt.

I ran into Bennie on the street as I was walking home from the hospital. I didn't even see him at first because I was so lost in my own thoughts of Amy and her cancer.

"Hey, Karen," he called to me. I looked up and saw him smiling with that crazy grin. "I've been walking next to you for half a block and you didn't even see me," he said.

"I've got a lot on my mind," I told

him. I wasn't ready to explain to him just what was bothering me so much.

"We're having a party at my place. Want to come? Looks to me like you could use some fun," Bennie said.

I was about to say no, and go right on home, when something held me back. I'd been staying away from parties ever since that time at Eric's. But there was something about going to a party that sounded good to me right then.

"C'mon, Karen. What's the hurry to get home?" he said.

He was right—there was nothing for me at home except chores and my brother's nasty looks.

Bennie had his own place, so the party was pretty wild. By midnight I had forgotten all my problems. The party gave me just what I needed—a chance to step out of my life and have fun. I got a real buzz out of the music, the kids, the booze—and Bennie.

I guess I should have known even then that he was bad news. We didn't talk very much, but it was enough. When I kissed him good night, I knew that I'd be back.

It didn't take long after that for Bennie to become part of my life. I started to drop by Bennie's place all the time. I'd often be feeling down when I got there, but Bennie had the ways to make me forget. I fell hard for him and his whole way of life.

I kept telling myself that Bennie loved me and I fooled myself into believing it. I told myself that the drugs weren't a problem, that they were only making a tough time a little easier. I told myself a lot of things, a lot of lies to cover the truth.

The truth was that I was split in two. I tried to be one person with Amy—the friend who could help her when she needed it most. I was another person with Bennie, but I'm too ashamed to say what kind of person that was.

But it wasn't until late in July that everything really fell apart. It was a hot, dry month and nothing had gone right. Amy was still in the hospital, more sick than ever. I knew that the chemo made Amy moody, but when she tried to lecture me for no good reason, I left the hospital so upset I wanted to cry.

I started to head home, but I changed
my mind. Maybe I thought Bennie could
cheer me up. Or maybe I was meant to
see what I saw there.

I walked into Bennie's place without
suspecting a thing. The front door was
never locked and I felt like the house was
mine anyhow. The place was so quiet
that I thought Bennie must be out. Then
I heard a noise from the living room—
and I knew what was going on.

Bennie was making out on the couch
with some girl I didn't even know. I stood
frozen in the doorway as Bennie turned

to look at me. I wanted to hit him and tear into the girl, yet something held me back.

Bennie started to say something, but I wouldn't let him finish. I screamed. I screamed as if somehow the sound of my voice would hurt him the way he was hurting me. Bennie and the girl both jumped up, looking at me as if I was right out of my mind.

I ran away before Bennie could get close to me. Tears streamed down my face as I fled from the house.

I ran down the street as if someone were chasing me, as if I could only save myself by somehow getting away. I wanted to get away from Bennie, from that whole part of my life, from everything. People stared at me as I ran along the street, but I didn't care any more. There was a wall between them and me and I knew they wouldn't cross over to my side of the wall and stop me.

As I reached the edge of the park, I waited, tired and out of breath. I knew then that I was running for no reason— no one was coming after me.

I felt confused and angry and awful,

all at once. I wiped the tears away and walked into the park. I made my way deep inside, way beyond the baseball diamond, until I found the spot where Amy and I used to talk after practice.

Amy used to sit on this big rock with her hands around her knees and I would lean up against a tree. We would talk about guys and school, about anything and everything.

Now Amy was close to her death, and I had no one but myself to talk to. I started crying again as I thought about how awful the world was. Overhead the sun was shining and the birds were singing, but I felt as if they were making fun of me. I wanted rain and wind to match my mood, but I couldn't even get that right.

There was nothing left for me. My family didn't care about me, Bennie had only been using me, and Amy would soon be gone.

That's when I made up my mind. And this time I knew I would do the job right. I had enough of Bennie's pills in my room to do it once and for all.

A funny sort of calm came over me

then. I began thinking, not so much
about me, but about my mother. I
remembered her the way she had been
years ago, when I was a kid. I saw her so
clearly it was almost as if she were still
alive. I saw her working in the garden
behind the house. She was waving to me,
smiling and friendly, almost as if she
were waiting for me.

I had loved my mother so much
when she was alive, yet I had pushed
her out of my mind. I really don't
know why. Somehow her death never
seemed real to me. I was always waiting

for her to come back and make everything right.

But of course she couldn't, I told myself, snapping out of the dream. The world was a rotten, unfair place and she was lucky enough to get out of it.

I got to my feet with all these thoughts still going through my mind. Somehow I could think of only one answer. I walked back through the park with blind eyes. I didn't see the sunshine or watch the kids playing baseball. I didn't want any of the happiness in life to weaken my willpower.

CHAPTER

My father was waiting for me at the house. "Karen, we've been trying to find you for hours," he said.

"What about?" I asked him. The only thought I had was to get past him.

"It's Amy," he said, looking at me in a way I couldn't understand just then. "Her mother called to say that it's ... well, it's almost all over. Amy's been asking to talk to you."

"Oh, no ...," I cried.

And then I was running again, running to the hospital, just hoping I'd get there in time.

When I reached the hospital, I saw Amy's parents standing in the hall talking to a nurse. Her brother was staring out a window, looking grim, and Eric was pacing up and down the floor. They all seemed to be waiting.

"Karen, I'm so glad you got here," Amy's mother said. "She's been asking for you ever since you left, but we couldn't get hold of you." She was trying to stay calm, but I could see that her hands were shaking.

"Is she that much worse?" I asked.

"She's going downhill very fast. We're afraid . . . well, the priest is with her now," she said, looking away.

One more shock—Amy was getting last rites. This was the end, the end of the battle she had fought for so long. I thought I would be ready for this moment when it came, but I wasn't. It doesn't matter how much you think about death before it happens, you're never ready for it. The fact that Amy would soon die sent a chill down my spine like a blast of frozen air.

I wanted to cry, but I couldn't lose control when everyone else was trying so hard to be strong. I also wanted to run. I was afraid to see Amy like this, at the very end.

The priest came out of the room and went to talk with Amy's parents. Her mother nodded to show that it was my time to go in.

There was no way I could avoid it now. Everyone was watching me, waiting for me to do the right thing and say good-bye to my friend. Somehow I was able to find the strength to go in. And the few minutes that followed changed my life.

Amy was lying in bed, hooked up to tubes and plastic bags and other awful things that hospitals stick into people. Beside her in the bed was the stuffed teddy bear I had given her for her sixteenth birthday.

Amy was so pale that her skin was almost the color of the bed sheets. In the last month, Amy had grown very thin. The skin on her face seemed to hang loosely on her cheeks. And her hair, the hair she didn't want to lose, had never grown back.

"Karen, is that you?" she asked. Her voice was weak and dry.

"Yes," I whispered, then repeated it louder so she could hear.

I moved over to the bed when I saw she was too weak to move her head to see me.

"I'm glad you came," she said, smiling at me. "I knew you'd come tomorrow, but... but that might not be soon enough and I had to talk to you."

Don't cry, I told myself, *don't break down.* I took her hand in mine and held it, trying to hold back my tears, not for myself, but for Amy.

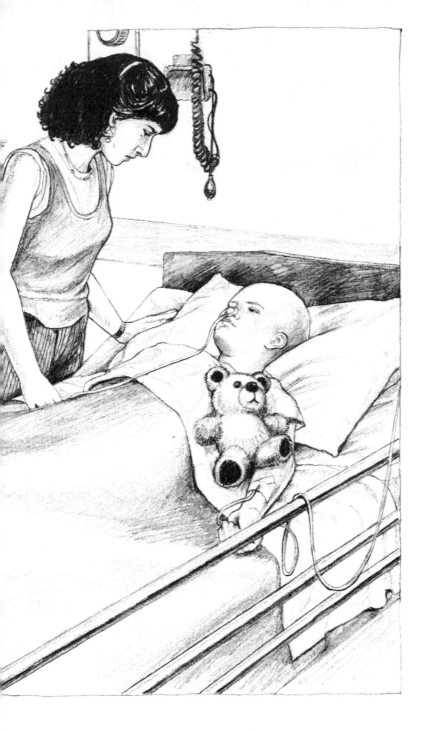

"I guess this is it," she went on. "The
doctors . . . they won't say anything, but I
knew when they sent for the priest."

She stopped for a second as if she
were trying to find some way to keep on
speaking. "The priest and I talked about
how I have to get ready . . . to leave all of
you."

I squeezed Amy's hand. I wanted to
tell her that it was all a mistake, that
tomorrow we'd both wake up from this
awful dream and that everything would
be fine. But that would have been a lie—
and this was no time for lies.

"Karen, I know you got angry when I tried to talk to you before—and I'm sorry. But I've got to tell you the truth now ... before they shoot me so full of drugs I won't be able to think any more." Her face twisted up in pain and her hand tightened against mine before she could go on.

"I want you to know," Amy said, "that you've always been my very best friend, even right up to now."

"I know that, Amy," I whispered, "you're really my only friend."

"Maybe we should start right there," Amy said, stopping a second to get her breath. "I'm not your only friend, Karen. There are lots of kids at school who like you ... who could care about you if you'd let them. You keep feeling so sorry for yourself because you think you're all alone, but you're not—nobody is. You have to learn who the good people are out there—"

I nodded.

"—and to stay away from the bad ones. This thing with Bennie can't keep going on. You deserve somebody better than that."

"I'm not seeing Bennie any more," I said. It wasn't the time to tell her about what had happened that afternoon.

"Good," Amy said, resting before she went on. "But you have to watch for the next one. There was Paul and then Bennie and then it'll be somebody else like that. What you tried to do at Eric's party, that was only the first time, you know. Bennie and his drugs, well, they're the second try . . . and then there'll be a third and a fourth until finally—"

She knew—she knew me better than I knew myself.

"And Karen," she went on, "that's such a waste. You are a wonderful, caring person . . . ."

Amy was crying now, crying about me. I held her hand as she lay near death, as the tears rolled down her cheeks. It wasn't her own fate that made Amy break down—it was mine.

"You have something to offer the world, Karen, and a lot to offer yourself —if you can just get over whatever it is inside you that makes you want to hurt yourself."

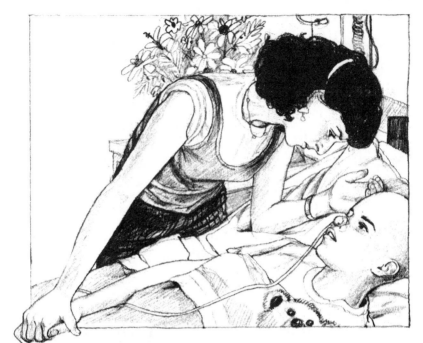

"But I don't know what it is," I said,
my voice cracking. I knew that she was
right. I knew that whatever was wrong
with me was all mixed up with my
mother's death and the way I felt about
my father and what I thought about
myself. But all that didn't make sense to
me, then.

"Karen, I can't keep on talking too
much longer. So listen closely to me,"
she said, her voice barely above a
whisper. "I want you to make me a
promise."

"Sure," I said. "Anything."

"I want you to go back to Dr. Vitucci until you find out what's eating you. I've got cancer, Karen, but it's in my blood and I know all about it. But you've got a cancer, too... except it's in your mind. You've got to get somebody to help to find out about it and get rid of it before it's too late. Do you see that?"

"Yes," I said. I was crying now because I couldn't hold back the tears any more. Because Amy was right and knew so much and was dying even as I held her hand.

"So promise you'll go back," she said.

"I promise to see the shrink again," I whispered.

"And now there's just one more thing," Amy said. "I won't ask you to make a promise because nobody can promise this for sure. It's more a kind of wish...."

I nodded because I couldn't speak.

"This is the end for me, Karen. I know I'll never get out of this bed and that... that makes me mad. I mean, it's not fair, is it? I'm sixteen and I'm never going to see seventeen or even sixteen and a half."

She stopped and the room was quiet.

"So after I'm gone, Karen, I want you to remember this—the next time you feel down and you want to give up on yourself, I want you to remember me here. I want you to remember that it wasn't fair. And then my wish is that you'll go ahead ... and live a little more of the life I'll never see. Will you do that for me?"

Her voice grew so weak I couldn't hear her any more.

"I will ... I promise," I whispered to her.

I don't know if Amy ever heard me. Her hand went limp in mine and her eyes closed. I knew even then that Amy's wish for me marked the end of her life.

CHAPTER

The two years since Amy died have not been easy. All I could do for her that last time at the hospital was hold her hand. When I think of all she's done for me, that doesn't seem like very much.

Somehow Amy's dying changed the way I thought about life. I spent a lot of time in the months after her funeral just thinking about that. Until Amy died, life had never meant much to me. It had seemed so easy, back in the fall, just to throw my life away. But the loss of Amy changed all that.

It was only after Amy died that I

began to see meaning in the life I was living. I learned that my life—every person's life—has value and purpose. That's part of what Amy taught me. Maybe that was part of her wish.

I called Dr. Vitucci right after the funeral because Amy had made me promise. I didn't understand just then how much I needed to talk to someone about all the feelings inside me. I guess Amy must have known how much I'd need help. And Amy had been right.

At first, I was seeing Dr. Vitucci twice a week because there was so much to say all at once. Somehow I had to deal with two deaths—my mother's and my best friend's. I didn't handle this very well.

My moods would swing up and down for no reason at all. For a long time it seemed as if my life were doubled up. When I was happy, I was twice as happy as I ought to be. When I was sad, I was sunk so deep that there seemed to be no way out.

I used to think this was crazy, but now I know better. I can see now that my being happy one day and crying the next were both ways to say good-bye to people I loved. The trick is to get through the low points in life, knowing that the high points will come again.

Dr. Vitucci showed me some ways to get through my awful moods. A nap, a shower, a run through the park, a talk with a friend—all of these things can help. If my feelings are really bad, I can call Dr. Vitucci or this hotline for people who are upset.

A few months after Amy's death, I even got my father to see Dr. Vitucci. My dad began to see that he was drinking too much, trying to hide from his own problems. At the same time, I saw that I wasn't giving him the help and support he had to have. We were both too caught up in ourselves to see what the other one needed. At least that much has changed.

I'm afraid that my brother is just the same. In fact, just last week I gave him a black eye for something he said that I can't repeat here. For once my father sided with me and said that Kevin deserved it. My brother then threatened to move out, which sounds great to me. I even think it will be good for him.

There's one other person who's important in my life right now, and that's Eric. He isn't my boyfriend or anything like that, just a friend-friend. After Amy died, we both needed someone to talk to, someone who understood our loss. So we turned to each other. Now Eric is almost as close to me as Amy once was.

Eric has a friend, John Sutton, who's been trying hard to make some moves on me, but I've been keeping him at a distance. I can see now that I've been

hanging too much of my own happiness on other people—the Pauls and the Bennies. I'm not going to do that any more. Dr. Vitucci says it's time to start enjoying life—my *own* life. And she's right. Amy didn't want me to live a life for her, she wanted me to go ahead and live a life for myself.

And I will—that's my promise.

About the Author

Paul Kropp lives in Hamilton, Ontario with his wife, Marsha, and their three sons. He began writing the books in the **Encounters Series** in 1978 while teaching special education at a local high school. He now has over a quarter million books in print, all dealing with the concerns of young adults.

If you enjoyed this book,
you might also enjoy reading...

BABY, BABY
When two people love each other, anything they do is all
right. That's what Dave tells Lori. But when Lori gets
pregnant, they find out that love is not enough.

FAIR PLAY
When Andy Singh asks Carol to a party, she couldn't care
less whether his skin is black or white. But her old
boyfriend cares far too much. His jealousy and hate lead
to a night of danger on the icy streets of Windsor.

RUNAWAY
Kathy wishes she were a goldfish. She has some good
reasons—her father gets drunk and beats her, her best
friend drives her crazy, and her boyfriend wants to get
too friendly. Will she be better off if she runs away?

WILD ONE
Kate saves Wild One from Banner's whip and gets to
train the horse herself. But that's only a start. Can she
prove he can race before it's too late?

How many books in the **Encounters Series** have you
read?

AMY'S WISH
BABY, BABY
BURN OUT
DEAD ON
DIRT BIKE
DOPE DEAL
FAIR PLAY
GANG WAR
HOT CARS
MICRO MAN
NO WAY
RUNAWAY
SNOW GHOST
SPIN OUT
THE BEAST
WILD ONE